Justin Adams

At the picket-line: A military drama of the Civil War

In five acts

Justin Adams

At the picket-line: A military drama of the Civil War
In five acts

ISBN/EAN: 9783337224554

Printed in Europe, USA, Canada, Australia, Japan

Cover: Foto ©Andreas Hilbeck / pixelio.de

More available books at **www.hansebooks.com**

A Military Drama of the Civil War, in Five Acts

BY

JUSTIN ADAMS

AUTHOR OF " T'RISS ; OR, BEYOND THE ROCKIES," " THE INFERNAL MACHINE,"
" DAWN," " THE SUICIDE CLUB," " THE ENGINEER," " THE
RAG-PICKER'S CHILD," " THE LIMIT OF
THE LAW," " DOWN EAST," ETC.

———————

BOSTON

1893

CHARACTERS.

CALEB HOLMES, *a wayward son.*

ALBERT CHERRINGTON, *a hero of the Rebellion.*

HARVEY CROSSCOMB, *a man of schemes.*

SQUIRE HOLMES, *rheumatic in body, but Roman in soul.*

HIRAM LUFKIN, *a raw recruit in love and war.*

JERRY SLATER, *a camp-follower.*

SERGEANT O'STOUT, U. S. A.

CAPT. HARFORD, *afterwards Colonel, U. S. A.*

DUMPY, *a soldier.*

DETECTIVE.

SILVY HOLMES, *sister, daughter, and sweetheart — faithful in all.*

LEONORA HARFORD, *a Union spy.*

SAL, *a camp-follower.*

SCENE PLOT.

Act I. Landscape in 4. Rustic fence or stone wall in 3, with opening c. Farm-house, L. 2 E.; barn, R.; stump, L.; saw and saw-horse with beam on it, R. General air of neglect and dilapidation.

Act II. SCENE I. Landscape in 4, with set rock R. and L. 3 E. SCENE II. Lane or street in I. SCENE III. Tent or officer's headquarters in 3, backed by landscape; flags, camp-stools, etc.

Act III. SCENE I. Rocky pass in 4, with run in 3. SCENE II. Dark wood in I. SCENE III. Same as Scene I, with dead bodies and débris.

Act IV. Union camp in 4. "A" tent down R.; tripod and fire up L.; mossy bank down L.

Act V. Kitchen in 3. Door L. F.; window R. F; fireplace R. Table and chairs L. Scene backed by landscape in 4.

PROPERTIES.

Act I. Saw, saw-horse, and log. Cane for Squire. Grease for saw.

Act II. Piece of string for Al. Guns for Dumpy and Hiram. Revolver (to fire), paper and pencil for O'Stout. Sword for Captain.

Act III. Two pistols for Leonora. Gun for Caleb (to fire). Pocket-book for dying soldier. Knife for Sal.

Act IV. Pipe and tobacco for O'Stout. Blanket to toss Hiram in. Large bottle, and small one for Caleb.

Act V. Armful of firewood for Squire. Cane for Squire. Ring for Cherrington.

COSTUMES.

Modern and military. Changes as indicated.

3

AT THE PICKET LINE.

ACT I.

SCENE. — *Landscape in 4. Rustic fence or stone wall in 3, with opening* C. *Farm-house*, L. 2 E. ; *barn*, R. ; *stump*, L. ; *saw and saw-horse, with log*, R. ; *general air of neglect and dilapidation.*

(*Enter* SILVY, *supporting* SQUIRE, R. U. E.)

SILVY. Easy ! Lean on me, pa. Here we are. (*She seats him on stump*, L.) There ! How does it feel now ?

SQUIRE. Not much better, Silvy ; perhaps it will limber up a bit after I've rested awhile. Come, sit down, child ; you must be tired yourself.

SILVY. Not a bit of it. Don't you know I've got my gate post to finish ?

SQUIRE. No, Silvy, you must not ; you are not accustomed to hard work, and I suffer almost as much from seeing you overtax yourself as I do from this confounded rheumatism.

SILVY. Overtax myself ! Why, pa, it makes me strong, and what we need about the place now is muscle. Just watch me. (*Crosses to saw*, R.)

SQUIRE. She's the best darter that ever lived. What would I do without her. Be careful, Silvy, and don't cut yourself.

SILVY. I guess this saw needs a little grease. Yes, and it needs resetting, too —its teeth are looking ten different ways for Sunday. I'll try a little grease. (*Exit into house.*)

SQUIRE. It's time Hiram was along with another load of hay.

(*Enter* HIRAM, R. U. E.)

HIRAM. Why, I thought I heerd Silvy's voice singing out as I came up the road. Wonder where she's gone to. Can't be milkin', 'cos there hain't nothin' on the farm to milk 'cept milkweed, and there's plenty o' that now since the Squire's been tuck with rheumatiz. Hullo ! somebody's been a sawin' for 'em. Wonder who 'twas. There ain't no men folks here but the Squire, and he's too lame. Wonder if Silvy's been a tryin' of it.

SQUIRE. Is that you, Hiram ?

HIRAM. It's me, Squire ; I came up tew — tew —

SQUIRE. You come to see Silvy, didn't you ?

HIRAM. Well, partly, and I kinder wanted to have a talk with you, tew. You see, Squire, my ma and Marthy Ellen they're kinder 'posed to the idea of my workin' for you for nothing, and leaving father to do all the work to home 'cept the chores.

SQUIRE. Well, Hiram, I'll pay you just as soon as I can. You know how tight run I am since this consarned rheumatiz took hold on me. I promised you ten dollars if you'd do my hayin' for me, and I calkerlate to be able to pay you.

HIRAM. Yes, but ma says if you'd halve it — give me five now, and t'other five when the rest on it's in — why 'twould kinder — kinder —

SQUIRE. Well, Hiram, I can't do it. Money's been so scarce, 'specially since the war broke out. If my boy Caleb was only here to help me —

HIRAM. Do you s'pose he's gone to the war ?

SQUIRE. I don't know, Hiram. I shouldn't be s'prised. He was always wild as a two-year-old, you know ; in fact, his wildness caused our fallin' out. That's the reason we split.

HIRAM. That was a bad day for you, Squire.

SQUIRE. No, it warn't ; not half as bad as the day Al Cherrington left me. He was more a son to me than my own. But I wouldn't forgive Caleb if he crawled to me on his hands and knees. That's the kind of a father I am.

SILVY (inside). Pa ! where's the grease ?

SQUIRE. There, do you hear that ? That's all I live for. If 'twan't for her, I'd just as lieve go.

HIRAM. You're not the only one, Squire, that's living for her sake. I kinder hanker that way myself.

SILVY (inside). Pa ! where's the grease ?

SQUIRE. What grease, Silvy ?

SILVY. The grease for the saw.

SQUIRE. In the pantry on the shelf. Well, Hiram, if you can wait a day or so, mebbe by that time I can give you the money. Neighbor Crosscomb's gone down to Boston on business, and I asked him to call on my brother-in-law and see if he'd loan me some money. We haven't been friends since I married his sister thirty years ago, and he may refuse ; but if you can't wait till then — why, we'll have to stop hayin'.

HIRAM. Well, Squire, it all depends on Silvy.

SQUIRE. How's that, Hi.

HIRAM. Well, if she'll only say one word, Squire, I'll do all the hayin' for both of you.

SQUIRE. O ho ! one word, eh ? Well, mebbe you'd better ask her to speak that word. Silvy !

SILVY. Well !

HIRAM. Not now, Squire.

SQUIRE. Why not ?

HIRAM. 'Cos I feel kinder skeered — kinder like puttin' it off.

SQUIRE (*aside*). I hope you will feel like puttin' it off till the hayin's done.

SILVY (*inside*). What did you want, pa ?

SQUIRE. Did you find the grease ?

SILVY (*inside*). Yes ; but it was all one cake.

HIRAM (*aside*). Just like me.

SILVY (*inside*). But it's soft now.

SQUIRE. Just like you, too, Hiram.

SILVY (*entering*). It's all right now. Hullo, Hi!

HIRAM. Hullo, Silvy. Kinder looks as though we were going to have a spell o' weather.

SILVY. Shouldn't be s'prised, Hi.

SQUIRE (*aside*). Guess I'll go in and give that word a chance. Hiram, I wish you'd hurry that word up a bit. That cloud out there looks pesky threatnin' for hay. (*Exit into house.*)

SILVY (*struggling with saw*). It just seems to me as though this saw's wood, and the wood's iron. I don't see how the men folks do this, unless it's the beer they drink that helps 'em.

HIRAM. Let me help you, Silvy.

SILVY. No, I won't. I said I'd make this gate post myself, and I'll do it if I raise that blister as big as a hen's egg.

HIRAM. You never let me do anything for you, Silvy.

SILVY. 'Cos you never want to unless you git paid for it. I heard you talking to pa, and I know what you were talking about, too.

HIRAM. Did you? Well, Silvy, I know I don't 'mount to much, but if you'll just say one little word, I'll jump right over the moon for you.

SILVY. Will you? Well, you just wait till the moon's full, and I'll give you a trial.

HIRAM. Couldn't you say it now, Silvy?

SILVY. Yes, I will, and I'll spell it, too, g-i-t o-u-t — git out.

HIRAM. Well, that ain't zactly the word I expected, so I guess I'll wait till the moon's full. (*Exit.*)

SILVY. That's number five I've said that to. The other four went to the war, but he won't. He's too much of a coward. I wonder if pa's lying down. I must fix his bed for him.

(*Exit, and enter* CALEB, L. U. E.)

CALEB. Poor little sister, what a life of sacrifice is hers, and what a contrast to mine. Yet, vagabond as I am, the memory of her love often calls me back to honor and to manhood. Shall I make myself known to her? Perhaps I'd better not, for were she to receive me coldly, I'd carry away more bitter memories than ever. Well, I can help her a trifle at least. (*Saws wood; enter* SILVY.)

SILVY. Here! you needn't think you're going to get paid for that.

CALEB (*aside*). The same sweet voice.

SILVY. You'd better make tracks out o' here. My father keeps a gun loaded for tramps.

CALEB (*aside*). I cannot resist. (*Aloud.*) Silvy!

SILVY. Is it Caleb? Yes, Caleb — my brother.

CALEB. Not too loud, Silvy, father may hear us.

SILVY. No, Caleb, father's asleep. But why not let him hear us ?
Why not come to him and ask forgiveness?

CALEB. Forgiveness for what? What have I done? Must I
crawl when an old man is testy, even tho' he is my father ? I but
asserted my rights in our quarrel two years ago. Must I play second fiddle to a waif he chose to foster as his son, and have a
foundling held up before me as a model?

SILVY. Don't, Caleb, don't say that of poor Al.

CALEB. Well, little sister, you are right in that. It was no fault
of Al's, and if left alone by father I could have loved Albert as a
brother.

SILVY. Could you, Caleb — I am so glad.

CALEB. Are you? And why?

SILVY. Because — because some day he may be your brother.

CALEB. Oho! Well, little sister, if this hand were mine to be-
stow, I truly think I could not give it to a better man.

SILVY. But you have not told me of yourself.

CALEB. Well, there is little to tell. You know my roving dis-
position ; it has led me over a good part of the world these past two
years.

SILVY. I hope it has not led you into evil.

CALEB. I cannot lay claim to being a saint, but this I can say —
I have used the world much better than the world has used me.

SQUIRE (*inside*). Silvy — is that Mr. Crosscomb?

SILVY. No, pa, it's —(CALEB *interposes*) not Mr. Crosscomb.

CALEB. I must go. I will remain in the neighborhood a few
days, and see you again.

SILVY. Caleb, do let me tell him you're here.

CALEB. No; not a word.

SILVY. Let me give him a hint.

CALEB. No, Silvy, you must not, but this you may do : you may
speak of me often to him, tell him what a help I would be in his in-
firmity, and perhaps he may relent. Now, darling, good-by. (*Kisses
her and exit.*)

SILVY. Poor brother, he does not know that pa has forbidden
me to even mention his name.

(*Enter* CROSSCOMB, L. U. E.)

CROSSCOMB. How do, Silvy.

SILVY. Oh, is it you, Mr. Crosscomb?

CROSSCOMB. Yes, Silvy, just from Boston. Ain't you glad to
see me?

SILVY. Oh, yes, I'm awful glad. Pa's in the sitting-room.
(*Aside.*) Hateful old thing,

CROSSCOMB. Where be you going, Silvy?

SILVY. I'm going to lock up the hen-house. (*Exit* R. I E.)

CROSSCOMB. That's a lie, for there are no hens there to need locking up. She's avoiding me, the little minx, but it won't be for long— it won't be for long. (*Enter* ALBERT CHERRINGTON, L. U. E.) What do I see? Is that you, Cherrington?

ALBERT. Why, Mr. Crosscomb, how are you? You look younger than you did three years ago.

CROSSCOMB. I feel it, too. But what brings you here?

ALBERT. Well, I had a few days to myself, so I thought I'd look up Mr. Holmes. He was very kind to me as a lad, you know. Besides, I want to acquaint him with a piece of good news.

CROSSCOMB. Good news is always welcome.

ALBERT. I imagine this will be to him. As I came through Boston I heard that his brother-in-law, Mr. Worthington, died intestate, and they are looking for the heirs.

CROSSCOMB (*aside*). This young hound knows it then, and may ruin all. I must see the Squire first and prepare the way. (*Aloud.*) It must be a mistake, for I just came from Boston and left Mr. Worthington in good health.

ALBERT. 'Twas merely a rumor. I'm sorry, however, it isn't true.

CROSSCOMB. Well, I came to see the Squire too, and as mine's business and yours is pleasure, you don't mind giving me first turn, I dare say.

ALBERT. Certainly not. You go in, and I'll take a stroll around. Doesn't look much like farming, this, from the looks of the yard.

CROSSCOMB. Melvin Holmes always was a man for muck — specially in the wrong place. Muck's money in the right place, but that's not at a man's door. Well, take your stroll, Cherrington, mebbe we'll meet again afore I go. (*Exit in house.*)

ALBERT. What can it mean, this aspect of poverty, where everything looks so neglected and bare? (*Enter* SILVY, R. I E.) What, Silvy!

SILVY. What, Albert is it you? (*Embrace.*) Don't kiss me, some one may be looking.

ALBERT. Let them look and envy me. (*Kisses her.*) Why, Silvy, what a woman you've grown to be. How you have changed.

SILVY. So has everything else since you went away.

ALBERT. I see they have, and I fear you are the only one that's changed for the better. Tell me — what is the matter? Where are all the farm-hands?

SILVY. All gone. We've given up keeping men, and it's a good thing, too. 'Twould be a shame to keep a lot of men about the place when pa's got a grown-up girl.

ALBERT. But who does the milking and so forth?

SILVY. I do — at least, I shall. We're not keeping cows now. Oh, I love to work. It's so much nicer than going to school.

ALBERT. Silvy, you can't cheat me. You're going to cry.

SILVY. I'm not. It's because I pinched myself with that saw.

ALBERT. What were you doing with that saw?

SILVY. I was making a new gate post. Don't look at me in that way, or I shall cry.

ALBERT. Silvy, I will look at you. I want you to answer me truthfully. Your father is my best friend. To him I owe everything, for he reared me as his own son, and if he is in trouble, I claim the right to know of it, and share it with him. Why didn't you mention this in your letters?

SILVY. I was waiting for things to mend. Poor father! I don't understand it. As soon as you left, everything seemed to go upside down. Pa was taken sick, the harvest was the worst ever known, and we had to sell all the stock for a song.

ALBERT. Good Heavens! this means ruin. But where is your brother Caleb?

SILVY. He was here a few moments since. Don't let pa hear his name. They quarrelled two years ago, and pa won't allow his name mentioned in the house.

ALBERT. Silvy, do you know why I have come here to-day?

SILVY. No — why?

ALBERT. To ask your father if he'll let me be his son indeed. He'll want one now that Caleb has gone. I have done well these three years in New York, and I think I could be not only a good husband to you, but a great help to him.

SILVY. And if he says yes, I suppose you'll marry me, whether I like it or not.

ALBERT. Exactly! You have no voice in the matter whatever. If he says yes, I shall go to Linfield to-morrow, purchase a ring, and shackle your little hand with it, as you long ago shackled my heart.

SILVY. Well, I suppose I'll have to put up with it.

ALBERT. And now, Silvy, which way did Caleb go?

SILVY. Down the road towards Holden.

ALBERT. Let us see if we can overtake him; perhaps by the time we return Mr. Crosscomb will have finished his business with your father and left him at liberty to decide our little matter.

SILVY. Little matter! I guess you'll find it'll be matter enough to keep your hands full.

(*Exit both* R. U. E.; *enter* SQUIRE *and* CROSSCOMB, L.)

SQUIRE. Now, neighbor, what news?

CROSSCOMB. Well, Squire, I've been to Boston for the first an last time. Never go to Boston. You'll drop more money there in a week than you'll git back out of a good crop in a bad year.

SQUIRE. Did you see the old man? There, you needn't tell me what he said. I know by your looks.

CROSSCOMB. Well, I did it all for the best, Squire. When I first struck there I heard that he was dead, but it wasn't so, Squire — it wasn't so.

SQUIRE. Even if he was, I don't suppose it would benefit me.

CROSSCOMB. But it might your children, for he was their uncle, and had none of his own. But no such good luck. There are a great many people by the name of Worthington. I looked him up. I spent half a dollar in finding him, which I did in a rotten old office on a rotten old wharf that you wouldn't put a pig in. I put the case to him just as if it was my own. " Old gentleman," says I, " there's honest Squire Holmes that married your sister, and is father to your own niece and nephew, that's come down to the bottom through sickness and the like of that, and here's you rollin' in your thousands that might pay off his honest debts and set him a-going agin with one stroke of your pen."

SQUIRE. I wish you'd told him that if 'twan't for Silvy's sake, afore I'd go beggin' of him, I'd see him in Jericho.

CROSSCOMB. " Well," says he, " you tell Melvin Holmes that when he married my sister agin my will, he knew what to expect. Tell him," and these were his very words, Squire, " tell him to go to the devil, and here's five cents to pay the toll."

SQUIRE. Well, I suppose it's all up now. That was the last chance I hoped for to lift your mortgage. I haven't forgotten that the last quarter's interest falls due to-day, and that I'm three months in arrears, so I s'pose there's nothing left for me to do but hand you the keys of the house and go.

CROSSCOMB. Why, I haven't foreclosed yet, and if I had, I wouldn't turn you out as if the house was afire. Where could you go?

SQUIRE. I'll find the lee of a haystack somewhere for me and Silvy. I'll carry away just my stick, the clothes I stand in and the girl. She's mine, and no mortgage can touch her.

CROSSCOMB. Come, come, Squire, hear me through. 'Tis true I can't afford to go without money or land. These war times are cruel hard. I can't, but I will.

SQUIRE. What! you will?

CROSSCOMB. I can't afford to, but I will — that's what I say. I'll take Silvy instead of both of 'em.

SQUIRE. You'll take Silvy? You'll take my little girl?

CROSSCOMB. Look here, neighbor; perhaps it may look odd, but I'd rather have Silvy for a wife without a cent than any other girl with a thousand dollars. It may seem like a fool's whim, but it's mine. I've watched her grow up from the cradle, and ever since she's been knee high to a grasshopper I've said to myself — that's the gal for me.

SQUIRE. Bless my soul alive! Does the girl know?

CROSSCOMB. Wal, a gal isn't blind to a chap's sweetness on her, I suppose.

SQUIRE. Why, man, you're old enough to be her father.

CROSSCOMB. Oh, no! not so bad as that. A man's as old as he feels, and I'm one of the wiry ones. I'm tolerably well off, and could afford to keep a wife. Besides, it's bad for a gal to be married to a young tom-fool that don't know his own mind. I know mine. I love Silvy, and you'd better keep the land.

SQUIRE. She's somewhere about the place. We'll see what she says to it. (*Calls.*) Silvy!

CROSSCOMB. I have your consent then?

SQUIRE. It all depends on Silvy.

(*Enter* SILVY *and* ALBERT, R. U. E.)

SILVY. Here I am, pa. Did you call?

ALBERT. Squire, I'm glad to see you.

SQUIRE. Why, Albert, is it you?

ALBERT. Yes, I've come back again like a bad penny. I should have come straight to you, but as Mr. Crosscomb wanted to see you first, I've told Silvy what I came to tell you, and she has promised to become my wife, if you will accept me as a son.

SQUIRE. I'm afraid it can't be.

ALBERT. Can't be, and why?

CROSSCOMB (*coughs*). I'll tell you why it can't be. Squire Holmes has just promised Silvy to another. Never mind who.

ALBERT. Silvy, do you understand?

CROSSCOMB. Young man, this is business, not sweet-hearting — she don't understand, but I do. She's got to save her father from ruination like a dutiful daughter, and she won't do it by marrying a struggling young clerk that's got to make his way in the world.

ALBERT. Squire, I have asked Silvy and she has said yes, so who's the other man? I have a right to know, and from you.

CROSSCOMB. It's enough for you to know, Mr. Cherrington, that Silvy will know her duty, and the Squire will keep his word.

ALBERT. And has it come to this — that Silvy is to be sold like the cattle? By Heaven, it shall not be!

CROSSCOMB. It's hard lines for you, Cherrington, but if Silvy marries you, the Squire must lose this farm, that's mortgaged stick and stone over head and ears. No, no! Silvy must marry money, and the Squire must keep the land.

ALBERT. A mortgage, eh? Everything is all right on that while the interest is paid. How much is due on that?

SQUIRE. Five hundred dollars and I can no more pay it than —

ALBERT. But I can, and twice that sum if needed. What's mine, Squire, is yours. You shall have the money and redeem the land.

CROSSCOMB. Too late! too late! He has given his word.

SILVY. But I haven't, and as I am to be bid for, I'll choose my purchaser. I don't know who the other is, and I don't want to know, but I'm going to marry Albert. Firstly, for the land and money, but mostly because I love him.

CURTAIN.

SECOND PICTURE.

CROSSCOMB (*shaking hands with* ALBERT). I wish you joy, sir.

ACT II.

SCENE I. — *Landscape in 4, with set rocks* R. *and* L. 3 E.

(*Enter* CROSSCOMB, R. U. E.)

CROSSCOMB. Ah, these scamps of soldiers! Thieves and rascals they are! They call it foraging, stealing an honest man's corn. But they leave to-morrow for the South, and my good riddance goes with them. Humph! Here comes young Cherrington, happy as a lark. How nice I deceived them! If they only knew the truth, that old Worthington is dead, and Silvy is an heiress, my chances would be small. Hang that young meddler, to turn up just·at the wrong time! But never mind, the game's not up yet. He'll not marry her for a while, and when he returns to New York, I'll manage to keep him there if I have to dig his grave myself, the young puppy! (*Enter* ALBERT, L. U. E.) Ah, Mr. Cherrington, you look as bright as a new dollar!

ALBERT. I feel so, too, and have good cause. I was just standing on the top of the hill watching the new regiment drill, and I thought what·a difference the future held for us. They, poor fellows, leave for the South to-morrow, many of them going to their death, while I — I am going to my life.

CROSSCOMB. To your life?

ALBERT. Yes, to Silvy; she's my life.

CROSSCOMB. Humph! You're taking chances same as they are. Matrimony at its best resembles a battlefield. It's a toss-up which side is victorious. Only instead of bullets and shells, you'll use boot-jacks and frying-pans.

ALBERT. Nonsense, Mr. Crosscomb! Silvy and I will use arbitration instead of either. But I'm glad I found you, for I wanted a word with you.

CROSSCOMB. Well, what's the word?

ALBERT. Why, it's this. I am to be married in a fortnight. Now you were the first to wish us joy, and I thought — perhaps — well, I know your time is precious, but I want you to spare a morning for once and be best man.

CROSSCOMB. What, I?

ALBERT. If you wouldn't mind. I can't send to New York, and all the fellows I know about here have gone to the war. Besides, you've been such a friend to Silvy and her father, that I'd rather have you than any other man. Come, say yes.

CROSSCOMB. Well then, I will.

ALBERT (*shaking his hand*). I knew you would, and some day I'll do as much for you. Oh, I forgot, a best man must be a bachelor. I say, Crosscomb, why don't you follow my example and get a Silvy of your own?

CROSSCOMB. Perhaps I will some day. So you're doing well there in the city, eh? Getting to be a rich man, are you?

ALBERT. Well, I've got my foot on the ladder. Fancy my coming back as I did, just in the nick of time. It looks like Providence, doesn't it? I wonder who the scoundrel was that wanted to buy my Silvy. I don't blame you for not mentioning his name, but I'd like you to tell him when you see him, before he tries to buy a girl at market again, to ask her if she wants to be sold. The cold-blooded brute! It makes my blood boil! For his own good, I hope I never shall learn his name, for I don't want to be bothered with having to lather a cur. But I'm off now to Linfield, and as I'm on "shanks' mare" I mustn't play by the wayside.

CROSSCOMB. To Linfield? On business?

ALBERT. Yes, and important business, too. I'm going to buy a ring.

CROSSCOMB. A ring?

ALBERT. Yes, *the* ring. Hullo! here she comes now with the Squire. Just in time to measure her finger.

(*Enter* SILVY *and* SQUIRE, R. U. E.)

SQUIRE. Al, your legs are younger than mine. Would you mind chasing them cows out of that pasture?

SILVY. Yes, we're poor enough now, and can't afford to pasture other people's critters.

CROSSCOMB. Why, whose cows are they, Squire? I don't seem to recognize 'em!

SQUIRE. Well, they're not mine, for it's a long day since my cows gave milk.

ALBERT. Why, they must be yours, Squire. The bars are all up. How could they get in?

CROSSCOMB (*aside*). I see it all. That young spendthrift bought them cows himself.

ALBERT. Why, Silvy, fancy a farmer's daughter not knowing her father's cows a hundred yards away.

SILVY. Al, don't joke about them.

ALBERT. Heaven forbid! Cows are much too serious things to joke about.

SILVY. Al Cherrington, you bought those cows yourself.

ALBERT. Take care, little girl, if you wrinkle your brows like that the cows may take fright, spread their wings, and fly away over the moon. You mind the milking, and never mind how things come. (*Crosses.*)

SQUIRE. Don't — don't be too good to us all. Don't ask me to thank you.

ALBERT. I'll only ask you never to mention it again. But I want Silvy to receipt the bill.

SILVY. How?

ALBERT. (*kisses her*). Thus!

SQUIRE (*to* CROSSCOMB). Come, neighbor, that receipt don't

need witnessing. Why, what's the matter? Come and take a look at the new live-stock.

CROSSCOMB. No, I'm very busy this morning. Good-day. (*Exit*, R. 1 E.)

SQUIRE. Why, what's got into him? Mebbe it's 'cos he's prided himself on having the best cattle around here, and he's afraid mine 'll beat 'em. Ha! ha! ha! He's jealous of my cattle! (*Aside.*) It's well they don't know I mean two-legged cattle, and that it's themselves he's jealous of. (*Exit*, L. 1 E.)

ALBERT. Now, Silvy, let me see your finger. No, not that one — the third of the left hand.

SILVY. What do you want of it?

ALBERT. Only its measurement. (*Measures with string.*) Now, then, I'm off to Linfield to buy that ring. I'm in a fearful hurry to shackle you. Good-by! I'll be back in twenty minutes. (*Exit*, R. 2 E.)

SILVY. Go the short cut behind the church. I'll wait for you on the hill. (*Exit*, L. U. E.)

(*Enter* CALEB, *from rock*, R.)

CALEB. I've given 'em the slip again. If I can only keep shady till to-morrow, I'm all right. They'll leave for the South without me, and I'll be two hundred dollars in pocket. I must get rid of this uniform and lay low. By Jove! here they come again! I must evaporate. (*Hides.*)

(*Enter* O'STOUT, HIRAM, *and* DUMPY, R. U. E.)

O'STOUT. Halt! Right face! Forward march! (*March down.*) Halt! Was it this way, Dumpy?

DUMPY. He was coming this way, sir, when I lost sight of him.

HIRAM. What kind of a looking chap was he?

DUMPY. A tall, gawky-looking fellow.

O'STOUT. That doesn't answer the description. There's nothing said about his being tall, and, begorra, he's no gawk, for he knew enough to light out when he got the money.

HIRAM. Was there anything said about his being short?

O'STOUT. Divil a word was said aither way. Here, Dumpy, you look that way and I'll look this way. (*They go up and* HIRAM *practises manual of arms.*) Look at that bogtrotter! I'll scare the divil within an inch of his life! (*Fires revolver;* HIRAM *drops gun and runs off*, R. 1 E.) After him, Dumpy, and bring him back. (*Exit* DUMPY.) There's bravery for you; the war won't last long if they're all like that fellow. (*Re-enter* DUMPY *and* HIRAM.)

HIRAM. Is the battle over?

O'STOUT. Where the divil were you running to?

HIRAM. I was practising a retreat.

O'STOUT. A fine soldier you'll make !

HIRAM. Well, I didn't 'list to be shot at.

O'STOUT. What did you enlist for?

HIRAM. For thirteen dollars a month and found.

O'STOUT. And a nice time they'll have finding you.

HIRAM. I had another reason, tew.

O'STOUT. What is it ?

HIRAM. Well, I was kinder sweet on a gal —

O'STOUT. And she shook you ?

HIRAM. No, I shook her.

O'STOUT. What for ?

HIRAM. 'Cos she was sweet on another feller.

O'STOUT. What did you enlist for, Dumpy?

DUMPY. I want to see the country.

O'STOUT. And what do you think I enlisted for ?

HIRAM. To get a pension.

O'STOUT. No ! Because I'm patriotic.

HIRAM. Most Pats are riotic.

O'STOUT. Come, now, let yez learn a thing or two. Attention !
Eyes right !

HIRAM *and* DUMPY. My eyes are all right.

O'STOUT. Attention ! Carry humps !

HIRAM. Who's she ?

O'STOUT. Who's who?

HIRAM. Carrie Humps.

O'STOUT. Attention ! Right shoulder shift arms ! (*They ex-
change guns.*) What are you doin'?

BOTH. Shifting arms.

O'STOUT. I'll shift yez into the guard-house ! Attention ! Present arms !

BOTH. Take 'em.

O'STOUT. What the divil are you doing now?

BOTH. Presenting arms.

O'STOUT. I'll present yez wid the toe of my boot ! Attention !
Rest arms ! (*They lie down.*) And what do you call that?

BOTH. Resting arms.

O'STOUT. Get up out of that ! Bedad, I'll have a nice job
getting yez ready for service. Now let yez try the song of the
regiment. (*Song and chorus introduced.*) Here ! Who's that
waving a flag of truce on that hill?

HIRAM. That's Silvy.

O'STOUT. And who's Silvy?

HIRAM. The gal I left behind me.

O'STOUT. Well, we must be looking up our bounty-jumper.
Here, Hiram, you're well acquainted with the lay of the land about
here, — you go that way, and we'll go this.

HIRAM. If I find him, can I try a shot at him?

O'STOUT. No; if you find him, march him to headquarters.
Now, Dumpy, attention ! Left face ! Forward march !

(Exeunt O'STOUT *and* DUMPY, L. 2 E., *and* HIRAM, R. U. E.;
Enter ALBERT, R. 1 E.)

ALBERT. Hullo ! There's a squad out searching for somebody.
It must be a deserter.

(Enter CALEB.)

CALEB. Hullo, Al, is that you?

ALBERT. Caleb, as I'm a sinner !

CALEB. Yes ; where's Silvy?

ALBERT. She's waiting on the hill for me. But what are you
doing in that coat?

CALEB. Oh, that's Uncle Sam's. I'm going to return it with
my compliments.

ALBERT. Why, do you belong to this recruiting regiment ?

CALEB. I did ; but I've taken French leave.

ALBERT. What do you mean?

CALEB. I've discharged myself. This is no time for detail. A
gentleman was drafted, and hired me as substitute. I enlisted,
pocketed the two hundred, and skipped.

ALBERT. You're a deserter, — a bounty-jumper !

CALEB. Exactly ; those are the technical terms.

ALBERT. And do you think you are acting honorably?

CALEB. Yes, honorably, but not sentimentally. I'd put on a
Confederate uniform to-morrow for the same price. What to me
is patriotism ! Merely a word which incites boys to risk their
lives for others' gain, while those fellows in Washington pull their
political wires and rake in the shekels over the dead soldier's body,
and the shrewd stay-at-home cries, " Bravo ! " and out of the very
nation's life-blood grabs a fortune at which posterity will point and
cry, " Behold the self-made man ! "

ALBERT. Well, Caleb, this is no time to argue politics. Here,
drop this uniform behind these rocks. They'll scarcely look for
them there. How comes it you haven't the regulation pants?

CALEB. Shortage in supplies. Uncle Sam begins to feel the
drain, and while some patriotic merchant haggles to get double the
price, the poor soldier must go without his pants.

ALBERT. Here, take my coat and hat. You'll be less conspic-
uous.

CALEB. Thanks, old fellow. I'll repay this service some day.

ALBERT. Now what do you propose doing ? Going to your father?

CALEB. Not much. Two years ago he turned me adrift and
left me to shift for myself. The row was all on your account, Al,
but I don't blame you ; I blame him for his pig-headed ideas about
a son's duty to a father. He never gave me half a chance.

ALBERT. And how have you fared since?

CALEB. Badly. I've tried everything under the sun but bank
robbing, and I never had a good chance to try that. I'm always

getting into a scrape, and it's generally through a woman or a horse. I always get the blame for others' blunders. If I was on Crusoe's island, I'd be in somebody else's scrape. If ever I'm hanged it will be in somebody else's shoes. I can't drink a glass of beer but it makes somebody else drunk; and if I went to this war I'd be hit with somebody else's bullet, and I'll bet a new hat St. Peter will mistake me, and throw me into somebody else's fire.

ALBERT. Well, Caleb, I must try and do something for you. Now listen. Loitering here is dangerous. Go straight to the hotel at Holden. Register there as John Smith, and Silvy and I will call on you to-night.

CALEB. Al, you're a brick. I'll follow your advice. You're only my foster brother now, but if what I hear is true, as Silvy's husband you'll be my brother indeed. I know you'll be good to her, Al. She's the best little girl in the world, and you're the best fellow. You're worthy of each other, and may God bless you both. (*Exit* R. I E.)

ALBERT. Poor Caleb! If I can only patch up that quarrel, it will be the happiest moment of my life.

(*Enter* O'STOUT *and* DUMPY, L. 2 E.)

O'STOUT. Halt, ye divil ye, halt! Surround him, Dumpy! Ah, ye blackguard, it's here ye are after keeping us trudging about in the boiling sun. (ALBERT *turns away*.) Aisy now — bedad, you'll not get away as aisy as you think.

ALBERT. Why, whom do you take me for?

O'STOUT. Take you for — for private Caleb Holmes, to be sure; and it strikes me you're rightly named, for you seem to like homes better than tents.

ALBERT (*aside*). Worse and worse! Cale has enlisted under his own name. I must go with them; it will give him more time to escape.

DUMPY. Here's his uniform, sergeant; I found it hidden there in the bushes.

O'STOUT. Aha! Look at that now. I knew it was him. You couldn't deceave me, if you tuk off your shirt. Come, right face! (ALBERT *turns* L.) Oho! by me soul, you're a poltroon. It's plain to see you were never under my drilling orders. Round the other way. Now then — forward march. (*All exeunt*, R. 2 E.)

SCENE II. — *Lane or street in* I.

(*Enter* O'STOUT, ALBERT *and* DUMPY, R. I E.)

ALBERT. One moment, my·friend!
O'STOUT. Halt! Front face!
ALBERT. Now, Mr. — what is your name, please?
O'STOUT. My name is O'Stout, sir — Sergeant O'Stout.

ALBERT. Well, Mr. O'Stout —

O'STOUT. I said I was a sergeant!

ALBERT. Indeed, I congratulate you. Well, Mr. —

O'STOUT. Do you want to exasperate me? I said I was a sergeant, and if you call me out of my title again, it'll go hard wid you.

ALBERT. Oh, you wish me to call you sergeant? Well, Sergeant, this mistake will inconvenience me a great deal. There's a young lady awaiting my coming.

O'STOUT. And as the regiment leaves to-morrow she may be an old lady before you come.

ALBERT. Well, Mr. O'Stout —

O'STOUT. I said I was a sergeant.

ALBERT. Excuse me — well, Corporal —

O'STOUT. Sergeant!

ALBERT. Well, Colonel! (O'STOUT *pleased*), if I prove that I am not Caleb Holmes, will you release me?

O'STOUT. Well, I'll consider it, but where's the proofs?

ALBERT (*aside*). Confound it! All my letters and papers are in my coat. The Squire must not know of this, or he'll never forgive Cale.

O'STOUT. Have you any friends who could swear to your identity?

ALBERT. I have, but they are all in New York.

O'STOUT. And before they could get here, we'll be in Dixie's land.

ALBERT. Stay, — I have a friend — Mr. Crosscomb — a respectable farmer. May I write him a short note, Corporal?

O'STOUT. Sergeant!

ALBERT. General. (O'STOUT *flattered*.) May I write him a short note?

O'STOUT. You may write him a dozen; but tell him to hurry up. (*Gives him pencil and paper.*) Dumpy, left face! Bend your back. Now write.

ALBERT (*writing on* DUMPY'S *back*). "Dear Crosscomb: A blundering Irish soldier " —

O'STOUT. Here! here! Cross that out, or I'll not lave you send it.

ALBERT. I beg pardon. "A distinguished military gentleman has arrested me for a deserter. I'm mistaken for another man, and the worst of the blunder is that the regiment is bound for the South to-morrow. Come over to Linfield, pray, at any trouble, for which you may reckon on my gratitude. Ask for " — whom shall I tell him to ask for?

O'STOUT. For Captain Harford.

ALBERT. "Ask for Captain Harford, and tell him that I am, yours most gratefully, Albert Cherrington."

O'STOUT. Dumpy, bend straight ag'in. Dumpy, I detail you to deliver that note.

ALBERT.   The next house to the bridge.   Ask for Harvey
Crosscomb.
DUMPY.   Harvey Crosscomb.   All right.   (*Is about to exit when*
O'STOUT *coughs*; DUMPY *turns and salutes him, then exit* R. I E.)
O'STOUT.   Left face!   Forward march.   (*Exeunt both*, L. I E.)

SCENE 3. — *Tent or officer's headquarters in 3, backed by landscape* ;
flags, camp-stools, etc., about.

(CAPTAIN HARFORD, O'STOUT, ALBERT, *and* SOLDIERS *discovered.*)

CAPTAIN.   Your report, Sergeant, and be quick.
O'STOUT.   Caleb Holmes, sir, of Company B, enlisted yesterday
and deserted to-day.   Found skulking in the woods by me.
ALBERT.   Appearances are against me, sir, I must admit; but
neither have I enlisted, nor is my name Caleb Holmes.   I am Albert
Cherrington, a land-surveyor of New York.
CAPTAIN.   The devil you are.
O'STOUT.   It's a wise recruit, Captain, that knows his own
name.
CAPTAIN.   Can you prove that you are not Caleb Holmes?
ALBERT.   Unfortunately my letters and papers were all in my
coat.
CAPTAIN.   And where is your coat?
O'STOUT.   Here, sir; we found it not ten paces from where we
found himself.
CAPTAIN.   Young man, this looks bad for you.
ALBERT.   I know it, sir; but I can only say I left my coat be-
hind, the weather being warm, while I went on a short errand.
CAPTAIN.   Are you willing to swear to the truth of your remarks?
ALBERT.   I should prefer not to.   I have sent for Mr. Crosscomb
to identify me.   His probity cannot be doubted.   Are you not will-
ing to take his word?   (*Enter* DUMPY *and* CROSSCOMB.)
DUMPY.   Captain!   (*He forgets to salute* ; O'STOUT *reminds
him.*)   This is the party the prisoner sent for.
CAPTAIN.   What is your name, sir?
CROSSCOMB.   Crosscomb!   Harvey Crosscomb!
CAPTAIN.   Mr. Crosscomb, we have made inquiries, and learn
that you are a respectable and a responsible man.   The prisoner
has been arrested on suspicion of being a deserter, and has sent for
you to identify him.   Can you tell us his name?
CROSSCOMB.   No, sir, I cannot!
ALBERT.   My God!   Crosscomb, this is no joking matter; what
do you mean?
CAPTAIN.   Remember, sir, his fate hangs on your answer.   The
penalty for desertion on the battlefield is death, and his will be
scarcely less.   Should you prove him guilty, he will be taken to the
dry Tortugas.

CROSSCOMB. I never saw that man before in all my life.
CAPTAIN. You swear it?
CROSSCOMB. I do.
ALBERT. I am lost!
CAPTAIN. Fall in.
ALBERT. Very well! If fate compels me to be a soldier, my first duty shall be to kill a traitor.

(*Snatches* CAPTAIN'S *sword and rushes at* CROSSCOMB ; *is held back by* O'STOUT *and* DUMPY.)

CURTAIN.

ACT III.

SCENE I. — *Rocky pass in* 4 *or* 5. *Set rocks* R. *and* L. U. E. *Set tree up* C. *Run at* 3.

(SAL *discovered seated on rock* L. ; *enter* JERRY, R.)

SAL. Well, what are they?
JERRY. The picket line of the Johnnies.
SAL. Johnnies — bah! They haven't a cent in the world. Come, let's make tracks away from here.
JERRY. No! While that New Hampshire regiment remains in this vicinity, I remain also.
SAL. Jerry, there's something in your noddle regarding that New Hampshire regiment. Come, out with it. No secrets from me, or we part company right here.
JERRY. Well, Sal, I'll tell you. There's a man in that regiment that I'm to get five hundred dollars for killing.
SAL. And who offers the reward?
JERRY. Never you mind ; but, then, I may as well tell you. Yes, I will, for I may get knocked over, and then the money would go to waste. My benefactor's name is Crosscomb, and he has a particular interest in this man's death.
SAL. Some girl scrape, I'll be bound. But have you located your man?
JERRY. Yes, I picked him out yesterday through a friend of mine. He 'listed under the name of Caleb Holmes. (*Sentry cries outside* R., "*Corporal of the guard, post ten — nine o'clock, and all's well.*")
SAL. Hush! come away. They may challenge us. (*Exeunt both* L. 2 E.)

(*Enter* CALEB L. U. E. *with rebel uniform on.*)

CALEB. I could swear I heard a human voice come from this direction. Where am I? I must reconnoitre. Ah! the Confederate picket line. I wonder whose command it is. It can't be my regiment — No, our camp is farther down the river. Confound this foraging, anyway. I haven't run across anything to eat yet — not so much as a bull-frog. But one must do it or starve. (*Horses' hoofs heard* L.) Hullo! What's this coming? (*Enter* LEONORA L. 2 E.) Halt! who comes there?

LEONORA. Why, monsieur, is that the way your most chivalrous nation receives a lady — at the point of the musket?

CALEB. Damme, if it isn't a woman, and a good-looking one, too.

LEONORA. Sir, I'm ashamed of your manners.

CALEB. And, by the Lord Harry, so am I.

LEONORA. Well, apropos of things at large—

CALEB. I'm afraid I must trouble you to show me your pass. Very sorry, but you see duty must be done.

LEONORA. Ah yes, duty! That's the soldier's word always. Pray excuse me, sir. Before duty, courtesy must yield. But what if I have no papers to show?

CALEB. Then it would be my painful — I mean my delightful duty to escort you to headquarters.

LEONORA. But suppose I mount my horse, and gallop away?

CALEB. I should follow on mine.

LEONORA. But suppose you did not catch me?

CALEB. But I would. Your horse isn't a patch on mine. But if you succeeded in getting away, I would simply raise my gun and shoot —

LEONORA. Me!

CALEB. Heaven forbid! Your horse. Besides, he would be good for beef in these hard times.

LEONORA. Then you would not harm me?

CALEB. Not for the whole Southern Confederacy.

LEONORA. It seems you do not value that very highly, and yet you wear the uniform.

CALEB. Force of circumstances.

LEONORA. What circumstances?

CALEB. You force me to acknowledge a weakness? Well, here goes. I was drinking wine one evening in Baltimore, and the next I found myself in this uniform, and that, after discarding a blue one but three months before.

LEONORA. And so you would shoot my horse for beef, eh? But what if I shoot first — not your horse, but you. (*Points pistol.*)

CALEB. Then you'd have to shoot, that's all. But I'm no good for beef, or anything else for that matter, and if death stared me in the face, I'd prefer his presentation from so pretty a hand as yours.

LEONORA. Now for that gallant speech you shall live. But the idea of a man who can say such pretty things being no good at all. I'm afraid you've had a great deal of practice, though you are so young. I am sorry you are so young, else I should ask you to advise me, for I am very unhappy spite of all I may seem.

CALEB. Oh! I may have young shoulders, but I've got an old head. I can give the best of advice, but I can seldom follow it.

LEONORA. You invite confidence, and you shall have it. Did you ever hear of Colonel Harford, that bravest of men, who was killed at Spottsylvania?

CALEB. Ay, Madam, he was the flower of the Confederate army.

LEONORA. I am his daughter. I have neither father, home, nor friends — the accursed Northerners have destroyed them all. I have just seen the torch applied to our old mansion, our slaves made contraband, our hearth-stone made the scene of plunder, pillage and bloodshed, and these are the men who are fighting for what they call a noble cause. It's a marvel that I escaped, not with life, but honor. I have ridden day and night; my last hope is to reach the Confederate lines and tell my story to General Lee, so that every Southerner, in taking revenge, may strike one blow for me.

CALEB. Yours is indeed a harrowing tale, but one of many contingent to this cruel war. But do you know your way to General Lee's headquarters?

LEONORA. I must hold by the river, I suppose; do you know?

CALEB. No more than the man in the moon. Do you know how far?

LEONORA. - No; how should I know?

CALEB. And you're all alone.

LEONORA. Entirely.

CALEB. Then we must find out where we are. I have been out foraging and have lost my way; so I'm as deeply in the mud as you are in the mire. I think my brigade is farther down the river. Here is the picket line at the edge of yonder wood. I know the countersign, and we'll find out. Come.

LEONORA. Stay! I cannot follow you. I must find General Lee to-night, if he is to be found; but the ceremony and delay through which I would have to pass should I follow you, would be very annoying. It is simple for you — you have strayed from your regiment and lost your way. They will give you the necessary information, then you can join me here, and we will proceed together.

CALEB. You are right, and that's something wonderful for a woman. I'll return immediately. (*Exit* R. 2 E.)

SENTRY (*outside* R.). Halt! Who comes there?

CALEB (*outside* R.). A friend.

SENTRY (*outside* R.). Advance, and give the countersign.

LEONORA. Yes, the word was right. He is through the line. Now to await the outcome of this adventure. (*Enter* SAL *and* JERRY R. U. E.) Ah, what have we here?

SAL. I tell you I'm sick of it. Here we've been following up this division for a week, and not the smallest chance of making a cent.

JERRY. It's all right, I say. The battle's bound to come, besides the mail has been cut off, and they have their pockets lined with money, so when it does come it'll be a harvest.

LEONORA. Camp followers! The brutal creatures who prey like vultures upon the fallen dead.

SAL. Sh! A woman, and alone.

JERRY. Yes, and well dressed, too. She may have diamonds. Easy now.

LEONORA. My heart sickens at the thought of the carnage that will redden this ground so soon. But it must be done — the nation must be saved.

SAL. Don't let her see you. I'll engage her from the front, while you steal up behind.

LEONORA. I wonder who my guide is. Poor honest fellow, he trusts the world as the world trusts him. I wonder if I shall ever see him again after to-night. I hope so.

SAL. I beg your pardon, Miss — wouldn't you like to buy some little trinket to give to the poor soldier you're waiting for?

LEONORA. No!

SAL. Don't your soldier boy use tobacco? See, I have some nice cigars.

LEONORA. I gave you my answer — go!

JERRY. Not yet, my lady. (*Seizes her.*)

LEONORA (*throws him off, and draws two pistols*). Stand back, you carrion dogs. Were it not for alarming yonder sentry, I'd shoot you both with less compunction than I would a brace of wolves. Go! your work is robbing the dead, and not the living.

JERRY. Come on, Sal, don't sneak that way. She dare not shoot.

LEONORA. Don't be too sure of that. Remember that one live woman is more dangerous than a hundred dead men. (*Exeunt* SAL *and* JERRY, L. 2 E.) What a pity I had to let them go; but the shot would have alarmed the sentry, and ruined all.

(*Enter* CALEB, R. 2 E.)

CALEB. It's all right.

LEONORA. Yes?

CALEB. General Lee's headquarters are two miles farther down the river, covered with earthworks and felled trees. This is an outpost of Mississippi infantry on the extreme right of the line. My division is on the extreme left, so you see I must have strayed four miles out of my way.

LEONORA. Rather a long line. How many men does it represent?

CALEB. About ninety thousand, to say nothing of the artillery which are posted on the hill two miles back from the river.

LEONORA. Ninety thousand? Good!

CALEB. But come — I promised to take you to the officer of the day. He'll provide us with passes, and then we may proceed.

LEONORA. One moment. Ninety thousand, with cavalry and artillery on the hill. General Lee in the centre. Right resting near the fork of the river, left four miles down the river. I thank you, *mon ami.*

CALEB. I've not guided you so badly after all.

LEONORA. You have guided me excellently, my friend, and I did right in coming to you for advice, so I will give you a little in return. Beware of a woman's tears, for they are seldom genuine. I like you because you are a good-natured, impulsive fool, who thinks of a woman before himself just because she pretends to cry. You are too good to be wasted on this barren cause. Choose then — will you forage and find thistles, or will you be a man and follow me?

CALEB. I see it all. Good Heavens! I have been blind. You are a Union spy.

LEONORA. I am; and if your heart beats true to the uniform you wear, I am your deadly foe. Come, dare you summon yonder sentinel and take me prisoner?

CALEB. Your sex protects you.

LEONORA. No; you dare not, for your heart is with the North.

CALEB. But my allegiance is with the South, and I dare and will defeat the purpose for which you mocked me with your woman's tears. You gained from my sympathy what the stake would never gain from my fears. But you shall not use that information. You are not yet inside the Union lines. I threatened if you played me false to kill your horse. You forgot your sex when you lied to me, but I do not forget my manhood when I fulfil my threat. (*Kneels and shoots* L.. *Horse falls outside* L.)

LEONORA (*draws pistols*). I thank you for emptying that gun. Surrender!

CALEB. What, to a woman?

LEONORA. Ay, a determined and desperate one. You said but now my horse was not a patch on yours. I will test that boast myself.

CALEB (*bugle call and drum roll outside* R.). That shot has alarmed the sentry; they will question me — I shall be condemned —

LEONORA. Ay, and likely hanged for giving information to the enemy. (*Looks off* L. U. E.) You were right, monsieur. My horse was not a patch on yours: and if he but carry me around the brow of yonder hill, I shall be in the Union lines, and use your information to advantage. May we meet again, *mon ami. Au revoir.* (*Exit* R. 3 E.; *noise of horses' hoofs dying away in the distance.*)

CALEB. The Union lines so near — then I am between two fires; but if I fall to the ground, it will be the first time that Satan ever deserted me. (*Exit* L., *as scene closes in.*)

SCENE II. — *Landscape in* I.

(*Enter* SAL *and* JERRY, L. ; *noise of battle in back.*)

SAL. Keep your eyes open now for stray shells, or you may get knocked into a cocked hat.

JERRY. All right, Sal ; the fight won't last long. I want to get my eye on that Caleb Holmes ; perhaps in the thick of it I may get a shot at him.

SAL. Which ever side wins, I don't care ; but I hope they'll follow up the retreat, and leave the dead to us.

JERRY. Yes. It will be bad for us if they bivouac. Let's get a little nearer. Keep your eye on the Fifteenth New Hampshire. Our game is in that regiment.

SAL. All right. I'll keep my eye on him, and on that five hundred dollars you're to get for killing him.

(*Exeunt* R. I E. ; *enter* HIRAM, L.)

HIRAM. By Jehosaphat ! they're thicker'n grasshoppers in a grain patch. They can't say I didn't stand my ground. I didn't run till I'd fired all my ammunition, but when I did run, I run like a son-of-a-gun. They say a good soldier never looks behind him. I'm darned sure I didn't till I got out of the reach of them sharp-shooters. Hullo, here comes a Johnnie skulking through the woods. I'll bet he's after me to take me prisoner. I'll just fool him. I won't sass him for I know a trick worth two of that. (*Lies down as if dead.*)

(*Enter* CALEB, L. I E.)

CALEB. Well, it's a woman and a horse this time. I'd better get a pair of long ears and pose for a jackass. (*Sees* HIRAM.) Hullo ! another unfortunate, hit by a sharp-shooter. (*Crosses* R. ; HIRAM *moves.*) What was that ? He still lives, poor fellow. (HIRAM *groans.*) Yes, he still lives, though mortally wounded. It would be a mercy for me to kill him and end his suffering —

HIRAM (*springing up*). Not by a darned sight. (*Exit* L. quickly.)

CALEB. Another poltroon like myself. My blood tingles to be in the midst of it, and yet I cannot. How glorious she looked as she held me there at bay. I've half a mind to plunge in and be taken prisoner. Perhaps I might meet her again. Hullo ! what's this regiment coming through the woods ; a New Hampshire regiment, as I'm alive. I can see their colors. They'll be met by Colonel Raleigh's horse. Yes, here they come. Now then, boys. Oh ! what a charge, and how bravely met. The horse retreat — the regiment follow ; but who's that brave young fellow staggering against the tree ? He is wounded, I can see his face. By Jove ! I know that man. (*Cheers outside* R.) Ah, the field is won. Another victory for the North. Now then, to crawl into a hole somewhere, and pull the hole in after me. (*Exit* R. I E.)

SCENE 3. —*Same as Scene* I, *but strewn with dead bodies, muskets, gun-carriages, etc.* CHERRINGTON *discovered* C.

ALBERT. Water! Water! What, am I dying here alone? Good-by forever, my earthly hopes. Curse the hand that struck me down. 'Twas not a soldier's, for I was facing the enemy. I dreamed that bullet sped way from the North — from Crosscomb's cruel hand. I can fancy I see him now, leading my Silvy to the altar. (*Vision through gauze drop at back, of* CROSSCOMB *with arm around* SILVY. *Her face turned away as if reluctantly giving consent. This may be omitted if desired.*) Yes, he has poisoned her heart towards me. Heed him not, Silvy — Silvy, hear me. I am coming — I am coming.

(*Vision fades and* ALBERT *faints; enter* SAL L. U. E. *She robs dead body.*)

SOLDIER (*as she robs him*). Whoever you are, I beg of you to send this to my poor old mother.
SAL (*taking pocket-book*). Yes, I will, and I'll send you to your mother earth. (*Stabs him.*)
SOLDIER. Ah! you she-devil.

(*Dies; enter* JERRY, R.)

JERRY. Is that you, Sal? What luck?
SAL. The best of luck. Did you kill your man?
JERRY. I hit him in the back, and I'm looking for him now to make sure he's dead.

(*Enter* CALEB, R. U. E. *unseen by others.*)

CALEB. And this is the end of all — friend and foe sleep side by side, their passions stilled forever. Some poor heart will ache for this one, some mother's tears be shed for that. (SAL *stabs another.*) My God! what's that? A woman robbing the dead and killing the dying? No, not a woman, but a fiend. (SAL *crosses to* ALBERT, C.; CALEB *steals up behind. She raises her knife to stab him*; CALEB *knocks it from her hand with gun.*) You she-devil!
JERRY. Leave the woman alone; the corpse belongs to her.
CALEB (*knocks him down with fist, then raises gun*). No; I'll not waste an honest bullet on you — go! (*Exeunt* SAL *and* JERRY L. I. E.; ALBERT *rising, the lime-light strikes him, and* CALEB *catches him as he faints again.*) My God! It's Al — my brother.

(*Enter* COLONEL HARFORD, SERGEANT O'STOUT, *and other soldiers* L. *and cross* R.)

COLONEL. What's this — a corpse robber?
O'STOUT. Yes, colonel, don't spare him — 'twould be a sin.

CALEB. Hear me, men, he is my brother.

COLONEL. A nice story that. You are right, sergeant, this crime demands summary vengeance — ready, aim !

(*Enter* LEONORA, R. 1 E.)

LEONORA. Hold! Colonel Harford, what are you about to do?

COLONEL. Kill a dog whom we found robbing the dead.

LEONORA. You are mistaken ; I know this man.

COLONEL. And whom do you say he is?

LEONORA. A friend to the cause. He is the man who gave me the information about the enemy. The man to whom we owe our victory to-day. (*Aside to* CALEB.) Hush! not a word. It is the only way to save your life.

COLONEL. His uniform is gray.

LEONORA. 'Tis but a ruse. His heart is white.

COLONEL. He is a rebel dog — ready! aim!

LEONORA. No! He is a Union spy.

CURTAIN.

ACT IV.

SCENE. — *The Union Camp. Soldiers discovered playing cards, others reading, writing letters, smoking, etc. "A" tent down R. ; tripod and fire up L ; mossy bank down L.*

O'STOUT. I say, Dumpy, this is mighty good weed you have here. Where did you get it? Did the wife send it to you?

DUMPY. No, Sergeant, I bought it from the old woman who came through the camp yesterday.

O'STOUT. Which pocket do you kape it in?

DUMPY. In my coat-pocket. Why?

O'STOUT. Faith, I'll kape my eye on you. In the next fight I'll push you in the way of a cannon-ball, and so fall heir to your tobacco. (*All laugh.*)

DUMPY. You might keep your eye on old Cummings too. They say he got something stronger than tobacco from the old woman.

O'STOUT. Was it a drop of the crater, Dumpy?

DUMPY. So I'm told.

O'STOUT. Will she be around agin to-day, Dumpy?

DUMPY. Yes, she promised to be around about this time.

O'STOUT. Come on, Dumpy, we'll see if we can find her. I need something to kape up my spirits. We've been lying here idle in camp so long that the cobwebs are forming in my throat.

JERRY(*entering* R.). I say, Dumpy. (DUMPY *stops*.) Doesn't it strike you as rather odd that one Caleb Holmes should be killed in the recent battle, and another of the same name should spring up to take his place?

DUMPY. Why, now that you speak of it, it does seem queer. But how did you know he was killed? You never saw him, for you only joined two weeks ago.

JERRY. I heard the boys speaking of the coincidence. They said you had a hand in his capture when he tried to desert.

DUMPY. So I did, and I've always regretted it, for I think we got the wrong man. But how does all this interest you?

JERRY. Why, you see, I came from the same township as Caleb Holmes, and I'm not sure which is which.

(*Enter* HIRAM, L.)

DUMPY. Here comes Hiram Lufkin. He's the very man to put you on the right track. He claims to come from the same place, too.

JERRY. Why, sure enough. Hullo, Hiram.

HIRAM. How do.

DUMPY. Well, I must be after the Sergeant to hunt up that female sutler. (*Exit* L.)

HIRAM. Let me see. Do I know you?

JERRY. Well, I don't know as we were ever formally introduced, but we're all comrades, you know. They tell me you're from Linfield, Hiram.

HIRAM. Yes, I be.

JERRY. Well, did you know this Caleb Holmes from there?

HIRAM. Yes, I did.

JERRY. Well, is this the same man who joined us a few days ago?

HIRAM. Yes, it is.

JERRY. Well, I wonder if he had an uncle named Worthington in the shipping business in Boston.

HIRAM. Yes, he did.

JERRY. He has a sister named Silvy, hasn't he?

HIRAM (*decidedly*). Yes, he has.

JERRY (*aside*). That's my game, without a doubt. (*Aloud*.) All right, Hiram. He's the man I thought he was. (*During above dialogue the soldiers have gradually strolled off* R. *and* L.)

HIRAM. What in thunder's he up tew? I don't believe *he* ever came from Linfield. They don't raise such murderous lookin' critters there. He tried putty hard to pump me, but he didn't make out to git much. Putty dry pumpin', I guess. The sucker would take hold. He ought to poured something into the pump

first. They think I'm putty gol darned green around here; but
they'll find out when the time comes I'll make things red.
VOICE (*outside* L.)   Hullo, hayseed.
HIRAM.   You go put your head to soak.
VOICE (*outside* R.).   Pumpkin head!
HIRAM.   You do the same.

(*Other voices from either side call out,* " *Jay,*" " *Reuben,*" " *Squash,*"
etc. ; four soldiers rush on with blanket, and toss HIRAM *in it.
Enter* CALEB *as Union soldier.*)

CALEB.   Hold on, there.   Leave him alone.   (*Four soldiers
exit.*)   What's the matter, Hi?
HIRAM (*on ground*).   Is that you, Cale?   Say, you ain't got a
mustard plaster in your pocket, have you?
CALEB.   Oh, you mustn't mind that, Hi.   They only do it to
break the dull monotony.
HIRAM.   Well, I guess they've broken my whole anatomy.   But,
Cale, I'm glad I've found you; I want to put you on your guard
agin that Jerry Slater.   He's been around here asking all sorts o'
questions, and gitting you mixed up with Al Cherrington.
CALEB.   Poor Al!   Why, what object can he have, Hiram!
HIRAM.   Gol darned if I know!   He wanted to know if your
uncle wa'n't in the shipping business in Boston.   He is, ain't he?
CALEB.   Yes, curse him.   He's as rich as a nabob, and a darn
sight meaner.   He wouldn't throw me a crust if I was starving for
it.   I don't want to know anything about him.   Come up to my
quarters, Hiram.   I've a newspaper from home   I've read it
through four times, now you may read it.   (*Exit,* R. U. E.)
HIRAM.   I'll commit it to memory like a Sabbath-skule lesson.
I will, by gosh.

(*Exit after* CALEB.   *Enter* JERRY *and* SAL, L. I E.)

JERRY.   We're in big luck, Sal.   I just got a letter from Crosscomb in answer to the one I sent.   (*Enter* LEONORA *at back and
listens.*)
LEONORA (*aside*).   The two camp followers I saw the night
before the battle.   The man must have enlisted, and for no good
object.   Perhaps he's a rebel spy.   I'll shadow him.   It will be
spy *versus* spy.   (*Gets behind tent.*)
JERRY.   Come into the tent here.   If anybody comes upon us
suddenly, we are driving a bargain over some trinket — you understand?
SAL.   Yes!   Now let's see the letter.
JERRY.   Here it is.   (*Reads.*)

" LINFIELD, N. H., Oct. 2.
Your letter informing me of your enlistment, also that of another
Caleb Holmes, came safely to hand.   From your description of the

man, he must be the brother of the girl I wish to marry, and co-heir with her to all the Worthington property. Keep your eye on him. Should he fall on the field of battle, as did the other Caleb Holmes, or die in camp of fever, *or any other cause*, I will do the same by you as I did before.

Yours,

HARVEY CROSSCOMB."

What do you think of that?

SAL. I think it won't do to wait for another battle. We may not be so successful.

JERRY. I agree with you, and have thought of a plan. Sell him a bottle of poisoned liquor. Mix it good and strong, so there will be no chance of failure.

SAL. But I must leave here directly after, or they may suspect.

JERRY. Yes, do so, and leave it to me to avert suspicion. Now go; somebody may be watching.

SAL. Don't you dare to play me false, or I'll serve you the same dose. (*Exit* L.)

JERRY. Now to settle this Caleb Holmes, and get the one thousand dollars. I wish a few more of the same name would turn up.

(Enter CALEB, L. U. E.

CALEB. Hullo, Jerry! Have you seen that old woman that peddles tobacco?

JERRY. Yes, I just left her. She's got something stronger than tobacco, too. (*Confidentially*.) Just give her the wink, and mention my name. I stand in with her. (*Exit* L.)

CALEB. Yes, I suspect as much.

(LEONORA comes from behind tent.)

LEONORA. Ah, my dear old simpleton, still looking for hooks to bite at.

CALEB. Madam, you never approach me but in the spirit of sarcasm. Did you save my life that you might have a butt for your stabs of irony?

LEONORA. Hush! my father.

(Enter COLONEL HARFORD, L.)

COLONEL HARFORD. Ah, my child, I have been looking for you for half an hour. (CALEB *salutes*.)

LEONORA. I have been to the hospital, reading to the poor fellows there.

COLONEL HARFORD. I might have known you were on some mission of goodness. Ah, my child, when I opposed your wish to serve your country, I little knew of what you were capable; but now I see that if this struggle results in victory to us, no little share of it will be due to the women who helped us on.

LEONORA. Nonsense, father; I shared your labor in peace, why not in war?

COLONEL HARFORD. Mr. Holmes, I have good news for you; you are to be made a corporal.

CALEB. I? Sir, I cannot find words to thank you. Believe me I do not deserve it.

LEONORA. Hush! (*Tries to catch his eye.*)

COLONEL HARFORD. More modesty. Need I tell you that your promotion was secured by my daughter? She told us how you donned the rebel gray that night, and in the face of the greatest danger learned the enemies' position. (LEONORA *signals to him to keep silent.*)

LEONORA (*laughing*). And how he nearly lost his life as a corpse robber.

COLONEL HARFORD. But come, Leonora, you are wanted at head-quarters. We have another expedition on foot that requires your services.

LEONORA. I will report soon, father. Just one word with Corporal Holmes first. (*Exit* COL. HARFORD, R.)

CALEB. Madam, how can I ever thank you — oh, I feel like a fool — no, a knave, after all my unworthiness to be treated like this. I have no right to the name of manhood. Why did you not let me die?

LEONORA. I saved your life because I liked you — you good-natured chucklehead! You are too harmless to die. Now listen! You are such a noody-noody, I will for the second time save your life. You had an uncle named Worthington who was very wealthy, did you not?

CALEB. I have. Yes.

LEONORA. No — you had. He is dead. You and your sister are his only heirs. For that reason certain parties conspire against your life. Some liquor will be offered you to buy. Do not let it pass your lips, for it is poisoned.

CALEB. What are you telling me?

LEONORA The truth. Obey me and you will defeat them. The same arm that struck your sister's lover down now seeks your life.

CALEB. Madam — Leonora — you are an angel! Whether your genius comes from the same divine source I know not; but this I *do* know — that all I have, even life itself, I owe to you, and 'twould be a sacrilege to repay the debt and be your equal. (*Kneels and kisses her hand.*)

LEONORA. Remember what I told you. (*Exit* R.)

CALEB. She loves me, and oh, how unworthy I am.

(*Enter* ᛡL, L. U. E., *with* SUPT. O'STOUT, HIRAM, JERRY, DUMPY, *and others, all clamoring for her wares.*)

O'STOUT. Aisy, now, ye spalpeens! Let yez have order, or I'll have the ould woman's privilege taken away, and the lot of yez put in the guard-house.

JERRY. No, boys, not one of you should spend a cent until he has squared himself.

ALL. That's so; that's so.

JERRY. He's drunk on all of us before to-day, now let him return the compliment.

CALEB. Of whom are you speaking, Slater?

JERRY. Of you. Why don't you set 'em up like a man?

CALEB. I'll set you upside down like a monkey. (*Rushes at him.*)

O'STOUT (*interfering*). Aisy now! The long and short of it is, the boys think, as you're lately appointed corporal, that you ought to celebrate the occasion by purchasing some of the ould lady's cough mixture.

HIRAM. Yes; we've all got bad colds. Ahem!

CALEB. Oh, well, as that's the general sentiment I will. How much, old lady?

SAL. Well, here's a large bottle that will go around the whole crowd. (CALEB *hands it to* O'STOUT.) And here's a small one for yourself alone. You may have the both for two dollars.

CALEB. All right. Cheap enough. Here's your money.

SAL. (*confidentially*). Don't give the others any out of the small bottle. It's superior. Drink it all yourself.

JERRY (*aside*). Now make tracks as quick as your legs will carry you.

SAL. Never fear. (*Exit* L. 1 E.)

CALEB. Now, boys, I have a proposition to make.

ALL. Hear! Hear!

CALEB. Well, as my friend Jerry Slater has insisted on my shouting here, and claims to be the injured party by my ungenerous habits, I propose that he shall take this small bottle and drink it all himself.

ALL. Yes! Yes!

JERRY. No, thank you; I decline. I'll drink with the boys.

CALEB. But I insist. You all heard what he said. I claim the right to dictate on my own shout.

O'STOUT. Yis, he must drink it, the blackguard, if it stretches him.

JERRY. No! no! (*Starts to run up* C.; *is caught and held by* DUMPY *and* HIRAM *while* CALEB *pours liquor down his throat; when released he staggers.*)

O'STOUT. Stand straight, you divil! Are you drunk so soon? (*He falls.*)

JERRY. Oh! I'm dying. Quick! an emetic! The liquor was poisoned.

O'STOUT. Poisoned! Don't stir to help him, boys. He knew it, and is caught in his own trap.

ALL. Yes, he knew it! Let him die! Down with him! (*They rush at him.*)

CALEB (*holding them back*). No! Don't touch him. Speak before it is too late. Tell me why you did it.

JERRY. Read this. (*Gives letter ; enter* COL. HARFORD, L. U. E.)
COL. HARFORD. Sergeant O'Stout, what is the meaning of this disturbance?
CALEB (*after reading letter hurriedly*). Speak — was it Crosscomb's work?
JERRY. Yes! (*Dies.*)
COL. HARFORD. Are you men to stand here and see a comrade die without assistance?
CALEB. They are men, Col. Harford, but he was not a comrade He was a snake in our midst, and, should they stir to save him, they would be no longer men.
COL. HARFORD. Who was he?
CALEB. He was the man who made his uniform a murderer's garb, who sought my life for greed of gold, and in the effort lost his own.
COL. HARFORD. What does that letter mean?
CALEB. It means that I, who have almost starved for a crust of bread, am now a millionnaire.

(*Picture of surprise.*)
CURTAIN.

ACT V.

SCENE. — SQUIRE HOLMES'S *kitchen in* 3. *Door,* L. F. ; *window,* R. F. ; *fireplace,* R. *Table and chairs,* L. *Scene backed by landscape in* 4.

(*Enter* HIRAM *at rise, with stick and bundle over shoulder.*)

HIRAM (*singing*). "Jerusalem, my happy — (*Calls.*) Squire ' (*Sings.*) How do I sigh for " — (*Calls.*) Squire! I wonder where the Squire is. Looks kind o' deserted around here. Kind o' like it did at "Hippopotamus" Courthouse, where Lee surrendered. Lor, won't they be s'prised to see me! But I mustn't tell 'em anything without orders from headquarters. I s'pose Silvy'll have a hundred questions to ask me about Al Cherrington. I wonder where they are. Guess I'll go up-stairs and see if I can find Silvy. "Jerusalem (*singing*), my happy — (*Calls.*) Silvy! How do I sigh for " — Silvy!

(*Exit* L. ; *enter* SQUIRE HOLMES, D. F., *with armful of wood. He is lame and decrepit.*)

SQUIRE (*dropping wood at fireplace,* R.). Well, I reckon that'll be enough to start it. It's getting putty chilly weather, and my rheumatiz is beginning to tell on me. It's hard work chopping

wood. Ah, well, I won't have to do it long. I'll have a son-in-
law to-morrow, and I'll make him do it. (*Sighs.*) Ah, poor
Silvy! But she'll be happy. Of course she will. Crosscomb's a
young man for his years. Of course not so young as that scape-
grace. Al Cherrington — no, I mustn't say that now, for he's dead.
(ALBERT *appears with army overcoat on at window, pale and
shattered in appearance.*) Dead like my poor boy Caleb. I'll
forgive them both, for now they sleep, perhaps side by side.
(*Sees* ALBERT.) Well, what do you want? (*Pause.*) Can't you
speak?

ALBERT (*perceiving he is not recognized*). I want nothing.
(*Exit* R.)

SQUIRE. Why, he's a soldier! (*Goes to door and calls.*) Here!
Come back! (*Coming down.*) It shall never be said that I turned
a soldier from my door. (*Enter* ALBERT, D. F.) So you're a
soldier, are you?

ALBERT. I have been a soldier. Don't you know me?

SQUIRE. Oh, yes; I'm sharp enough. I knew you were a soldier by your clothes. A soldier, eh? Ah, sir, soldier is a sad
word to me. A sad one, but a proud one. I had a boy a soldier,
but not a common one like you. No, sir; he was an officer.
Think of that, my man, an officer!

ALBERT. Good Heaven! He must mean me.

SQUIRE. Ah! I thought that would take your breath away.
Yes, sir; you're now talking to a lieutenant's father. Poor Cale!
He was always wildish as a lad. Too much like the old block, I'm
afraid, when the old block was new. But he died, sir — he died.
(*Weeps.*)

ALBERT. Died? How do you know?

SQUIRE. Oh, I know it — I know it. Neighbor Crosscomb
went to Boston and found out all about it. Killed at Ream's
Station.

ALBERT. Ream's Station! Why, I was there!

SQUIRE (*rising*). Bless my soul! Were you? Give me your
hand. (*Shakes hands.*)

ALBERT. And Mr. Crosscomb told you he was killed?

SQUIRE. Yes; and t'other one too. My foster-son, Albert
Cherrington. But he died on the rebel side, so I'm not so sorry
for him. He was a viper, sir — a snake that I had fostered. Crosscomb learned all about it. Why, what makes you look so sad and
queer? Dash it, you're a hero if you were there. Maybe — I
was his father you know — maybe you knew my boy. Maybe you
saw him die.

ALBERT (*aside*). Crosscomb! I see it all. What hellish vil-
lany! (*Aloud.*) What shall I say? Mr. Holmes —

SQUIRE. Yes; that was his name — Lieutenant Caleb Holmes.
Did you know him?

ALBERT (*aside*). This is terrible. (*Aloud.*) What was his
regiment?

SQUIRE. Eh? Well, that's slipped my mind. But my girl will know. I wish he could have been buried by his mother's side, but God's will be done. Churchyard or battlefield, it's all one to him now ; and I will meet him and forgive him, and he me, too, just as soon — just as soon — (*Weeps.*)

ALBERT (*aside*). His reason is leaving him. (*Aloud.*) Mr. Holmes, look at me. Don't you know me?

SQUIRE. Yes, yes — I know — I know. You were with my boy. He wore a coat like yours. But you shall tell us all about it. That is, if you don't mind seein' a gal cry a little. Yes, you shall tell Silvy and me. You haven't seen Silvy? She's terribly like him now and then. We'll be all alone. Crosscomb won't come for an hour yet, and I like to have her all alone to myself all I can now, for she's going to be married so soon.

ALBERT. Married!

SQUIRE. Yes ; to Harvey Crosscomb, the best farmer in these parts — 'cept me. They're going to be married to-day ; but he won't be here for an hour yet.

ALBERT. Your daughter is going to marry Harvey Crosscomb?

SQUIRE. Ay, in one hour, at yonder church, beside which her poor mother is buried. Ah, it seems but yesterday that I married her, and her brother has never forgiven her, and now he's rolling in his millions, and wouldn't throw me a cent to keep me from starving.

ALBERT. And she — Silvy? Does she love this Crosscomb?

SQUIRE (*rising*). Young man, if you weren't my son's comrade, I'd — why, of course, she loves him. But you shall tell us that story. I'll call her. Silvy!

ALBERT. No! Let her stay. What mockery it is that I had not truly died. The star that lighted my wretched life will shine no more for me, and this ring that was to bind us soul to soul shall curse an honest hand no more. (*Takes ring from hand, goes to window*, R. F., *and throws ring out.*) Away with it! Its use is gone forever. Would that I were in the trenches at Petersburg, or that the bullet that struck me had taken a truer course and ended my wretched life. (*Exit*, D. F.)

SQUIRE. Well, that young man is rather unaccommodating. (*Enter* HIRAM, L.)

HIRAM. Hullo, Squire.

SQUIRE. Who is it?

HIRAM. It's me, Squire. I've come back covered with glory, but no scars.

SQUIRE. Ah! My boy would have had them to point to with pride, but they killed him — they killed him.

HIRAM. Don't you know me, Squire? Don't you know Hi — ram?

SQUIRE. Not — not Hiram Lufkin? He's gone to the war.

HIRAM. But the war's over now, and he's come back.

SQUIRE.· Yes ; why, Hiram, it is you! (HIRAM *grasps his hand, and dances with glee.*)

(Enter CROSSCOMB, *dressed for wedding.)*

SQUIRE. Perhaps you —

CROSSCOMB. Hullo, Squire! Why, Hiram, is that you? (*Holds out hand to* HIRAM, *who puts both his hands deliberately behind his back.*)

HIRAM. Yes, it's me — all's left of me.

CROSSCOMB. You seem to have all your arms and legs.

HIRAM. Yes; but I'm missin' my wits. Them was skeered clean out o' me.

CROSSCOMB. You always were missing them.

SQUIRE. But, Hiram, you haven't told me — did you see **my** boy Caleb?

HIRAM. No; but I saw one of Mr. Crosscomb's friends.

CROSSCOMB. Who was it?

HIRAM. A gentleman by the name of Slater — Jerry Slater.

CROSSCOMB. I don't know him.

HIRAM. Well, he knowed you. I was present at his deathbed, and he sent his dying love to you.

CROSSCOMB (*aside*). This young devil knows something. I must hurry matters. (*Aside.*) At what battle did he die?

HIRAM. Battle — he wa'n't in no battle. He was pizened. He spoke about a Boston gentleman named Worthington.

SQUIRE. Worthington? Why, that's my brother-in-law — the mean old skunk. (*Enter* SILVY, L.; CROSSCOMB *holds out his arms to her; she pays no attention, but passes him, and goes to* HIRAM.)

SILVY. Hiram, is it you?

HIRAM. It's me, Silvy. (*They embrace.*)

CROSSCOMB. Ahem, Silvy! Remember we are to be married soon, and such conduct don't look exactly —

SILVY (*holding* HIRAM'S *hand*). Oh, I couldn't help it; I was so glad to see him. O Hiram, you must sit down with me for an hour or two, and tell me all about it. Oh, I forgot, I have an engagement in an hour. I must go to church and be married. But after that —

HIRAM. All right, Silvy; I've got whole bushels to tell you.

SILVY. Oh, I wish I had time to listen now.

CROSSCOMB. Come, Silvy, we must soon start.

SILVY. Mr. Crosscomb, before marrying you I want to say one thing, — if Albert Cherrington had lived, I never would have consented to this, even to save my father. I cannot swear to love you, only with my lips; but if you want no more than a wife who will simply do her duty by you, then for poor father's sake —

CROSSCOMB. Say no more. Of course I don't look to your loving me all in a minute as I love you. That will come in time. (*Aside.*) I know what I want.

SILVY. You have been very kind to father and to me.

CROSSCOMB. And I'll be kinder before I'm done.

SILVY. You will be quite content, then, with what I can give you, and will expect no more ?

CROSSCOMB. Why, bless the gal, yes. It is understood. Come, we'll seal it with a kiss.

SILVY. No! No! (*Shrinking in disgust.*) Wait till we are married. (*Aside.*) Oh! how shall I ever bear it ?

CROSSCOMB. See, darling, I was just about to buy a ring at the jeweller's, when coming up the road I saw something sparkling in the sun. I picked it up, and what should it be but a gold ring. You see fortune is on our side, for she saved me the expense of buying one. There is something engraven on the inside, but my eyes are too old to make it out. Perhaps you can.

SILVY (*taking ring and reading*). "From Al to Silvy." (*Excitedly.*) Ah it is *his* ring!

CROSSCOMB. Whose ring ?

SILVY. Al Cherrington's. What does it mean ?

CROSSCOMB. Nonsense, Silvy, he is dead!

SILVY. He is not dead, or that ring would have been buried with him. He is living — he is living!

HIRAM (*throwing down hat emphatically*). Yes, Silvy, he *is* a-living.

SILVY. Where is he — where is he ?

ALBERT (*entering quickly*). Here!

SILVY. Thank God — thank God! (*Rushes into his arms. After applause,* HIRAM *thumbs nose at* CROSSCOMB.)

ALBERT. Silvy, I know all now. I know whatever *seems*, that in your soul you are true to me.

SILVY. Ah, could you doubt ? Your faith is not as strong as mine, even when I thought you dead.

CROSSCOMB. Have that blackguard soldier turned out-of-doors.

ALBERT (*advancing to* CROSSCOMB, *who retreats behind table* R.). Mr. Crosscomb, you are the man who sought to destroy my life by a contemptible plot. You are too old and too degraded to horsewhip ; be off with you, and leave my own to me.

CROSSCOMB. Perhaps you think it's very noble and grand to come here a beggar, and bully a girl into sending her father to the poorhouse. Perhaps you'll pay me that fifteen hundred dollars he owes me.

ALBERT. You have made good use of your time, haven't you? When I left here two years ago the debt was only five hundred.

CROSSCOMB. No matter what it *was*. Her father now owes me fifteen hundred dollars.

(*Enter* CALEB, *nicely dressed.*)

CALEB. Then her father's son will pay it.
HIRAM. Hooray! (*Throws hat up.*)
SILVY. Caleb, my brother! (*Kisses him.*)
CALEB. Father!

SQUIRE. My boy — my boy! (*Embraces him.*)

CALEB. Father, I will save you, for I am now a rich man. After my discharge from the army, I went to find my Uncle Worthington —

SQUIRE. Yes, I know — a skinflint. The hardest-hearted old miser.

CALEB. Don't say that, father. The poor old fellow is dead. Died without a will, and Silvy and I, being the next of kin, we must divide a fortune.

SQUIRE. No, he is not dead. There is some mistake. Crosscomb saw him since that time. It can't be.

CALEB. It can be, and is. Crosscomb knew it all. That's the reason he wanted to marry Silvy.

SQUIRE. What's this you're telling me?

CALEB. That he knew it four years ago. That he tried to kill one heir and marry the other; but his accomplice was caught in his own trap and confessed.

HIRAM. And I can swear to it, for I was there. (*Enter* LEONORA, *well dressed*, D. F.)

LEONORA. And so was I.

SQUIRE (*crosses stage to* CROSSCOMB, L.). You gol darned old skunk, you! (*Strikes at him with cane;* CROSSCOMB *dodges and cane strikes table.* SQUIRE *strikes again; he dodges again, and is caught by policeman, who enters* D. F.)

POLICE. You're just the man I want. (*Seizes him and exit with him,* D. F.)

SQUIRE. Why, Caleb, who is this lady?

CALEB. This lady is your daughter.

SILVY (*kissing her*). My sister?

CALEB. Yes; and my wife. (HIRAM *dances with joy.*)

CURTAIN.

www.ingramcontent.com/pod-product-compliance
Lightning Source LLC
Chambersburg PA
CBHW030913260626
47169CB00008B/2833